Bats in the Graveyard

A novel by

Sharon Jennings

HIP-JR.

HIP Junior
Copyright © 2006 by Sharon Jennings

Library and Archives Canada Cataloguing in Publication

Jennings, Sharon
Bats in the graveyard / Sharon Jennings.

(HIP jr)
ISBN 1-897039-18-2

I. Title. II. Series.

PS8569.E563B375 2006   jC813'.54   C2006-903372-2

General editor: Paul Kropp
Text design and typesetting: Laura Brady
Illustrations drawn by: Kalle Malloy
Cover design: Robert Corrigan

1 2 3 4 5 6 7   06 07 08 09 10

Printed and bound in Canada

High Interest Publishing is an imprint of the
Chestnut Publishing Group

Sam and Simon (the "Bat Gang") have been friends ever since grade two. In their last HIP Jr. novel, *Bats Past Midnight*, Sam and Simon used a police horse to chase down a drug dealer. In this Bats novel, they end up getting trapped in a graveyard on Halloween night.

CHAPTER 1

Lost: A Green Sister

"You're really ugly," I said. I was looking at my little sister, Ellen.

"Really, Sam?" she asked.

"Yes," I replied. "You are really, really ugly."

I looked at Ellen's green face, the wart on her nose, her black teeth. She even had a spider in her hair. Yes, my sister was really, really ugly.

I had to hand it to her. All of Ellen's friends wanted to be pretty on Halloween. They went out dressed up as a bride or a princess. But not my

sister. Every year she wanted to be something scary. This year she was a witch. She was such a cool witch that I didn't mind walking her to school.

"Come on, let's go," I said.

I checked out the other kids on the way. There were some great costumes. I mean, one kid was dressed up like a Coke bottle. But there were some really stupid ones, too. I mean, who wants to go out as a strawberry?

I saw a kid dressed as a clown. *Boring*, I thought. But then he turned around and wow! He was a clown who got stabbed through the heart. There was gore and blood dripping down his outfit. Way cool!

It all made me feel sad that I was too old for this stuff. Kids in grade six, like me, we don't go out trick or treating anymore. Right? Too bad, because I could use all the candy.

We were almost at the school when Ellen took my hand.

"What are you doing?!" I shouted at her.

"You have to hold my hand crossing the street," Ellen said.

"Do not!"

"Do too! Mom said!"

I made a face and grabbed her hand. Then I took her across the street as fast as her little green legs could go.

"There. Now get lost," I told her.

"See you after school," Ellen shouted at me.

I was hoping no one had seen me with Ellen, but I was wrong. There was Jim Brody, staring at me. Jim is this big mouth kid who thinks he's funny. He's always giving me grief over something. Today the grief would be about Ellen.

"Hey! Who's the witch you were holding hands with?" shouted Jim Brody.

"It's his girlfriend," shouted someone else.

"No way. She's too pretty to be his girlfriend," replied Jim Brody.

"Sam's such a loser he doesn't have a girlfriend!"

Then all the guys started laughing. I could feel my face go red and even my ears felt warm.

I looked around to see who I could beat up. That's when I saw my best friend Simon. I mean, my *ex* best friend. Simon was laughing, too.

I walked over and punched his arm.

"So what are you laughing about, four eyes?" I grumbled.

"Aw, come on, Sam. Don't get mad," answered Simon. "You and Ellen holding hands — now *that* is funny."

"I was NOT holding hands with my sister!" I shouted.

I tried to explain, but no one wanted to listen. When guys get hold of something like this, they don't let go. So at recess, I got into a fight. I ran up behind Jim Brody and pushed him down. Then someone pushed me and three of us rolled around on the ground. Jim punched me in the nose and I saw some blood before I whacked him in the eye. Then some other kid kicked me and I fell down and split my lip.

Of course a teacher had to get all nosy and butt in. Mr. Chong ran up to us and started yelling. Pretty soon, he hauled the three of us inside.

We all ended up in the office for the rest of the

afternoon. Then the principal got around to us after the home bell rang at 3:30. He did his basic lecture about fighting. Blah, blah, blah. I've heard it a million times. Then he let us go.

I went looking for Simon. He's supposed to be my best friend. Where was he when the going got tough? The tough are supposed to get going, but Simon chickened out on me. Now he'd gone home without me. *This is a friend?* I asked myself.

When I got home, my mom took a good look

at me. This is not a good thing. I knew what was coming — another lecture about fighting.

But I was wrong.

"Where's Ellen?" she asked.

"Ellen?" I said.

"Ellen. You know, your little sister — about this high, dark hair?"

Very funny.

"I *know* who Ellen is, Mom. But why should I know where she is?" I asked her.

Mom just gave me this look. "Because you were supposed to bring her home from school, Sam."

Uh-oh.

My mom phoned the school and then jumped in her car. I cleaned up and waited for her to get back. I didn't want to, but just before she left, my mom said, "Just you wait till I get back!"

So I waited. Ellen got out of the car. I could see she'd been crying because the green paint on her face was a mess.

"I'm sorry, Ellen," I said. "It was just a mistake, honest."

Ellen kicked me in the shin as she went past.

"Ow!" I yelled. "Mom! Did you see that? Do something!"

"Oh, I will," said my mom. "But not to Ellen. To you, Sam."

"Me?"

"Yes, you. I've come up with the perfect punishment. I'm putting you in charge of Ellen's birthday party this weekend."

"What?!"

"There'll be ten little girls and it's a Halloween party," my mom said. "I want you to come up with things for them to do."

I rolled my eyes. "Ten girls . . . Halloween," I mumbled.

"Do a good job, Sam," said my mom. "Or else."

CHAPTER 2

I Vant to Drink *Your* Blood

I found Simon in the Bat House. This wasn't a real bat house. It's this climber in Simon's backyard that we fixed up and called the Bat House. That was back when we were little kids. That was the summer Simon moved in behind my house. Pretty soon, we became best friends. We called ourselves the Bats. We had a secret code and a secret handshake and stuff. I guess all that would have been really lame but we caught some crooks a couple of times. Then we got our picture in the newspaper. We were in the paper four times, if you really want to know. The last time was just last month. Some creep was selling drugs near our school. Simon and I caught him. Anyhow, we're still the Bats and we hang out at the Bat House.

Simon stuck his head out of the Bat House. "Are you okay?" he asked.

"No. I'm not okay," I told him. "I've got a fat lip. I have to spend a week staying late after school. And my cruddy friend didn't help me out."

"Sorry. You know I don't like blood."

I gave him a dirty look. Then I gave him my idea. "Well, don't worry, Simon, my man. I know how you can make it up to me." I told him about Ellen's birthday party. "And you're going to help me put it all together," I said.

"Sounds like fun!" Simon said.

"Fun?! Are you nuts?! There's going to be ten dopey girls there. We have to find stuff for them to do."

"No problem, Sam. I just read something about Halloween parties. I've got lots of ideas."

I rolled my eyes. Simon made a face. Then he

told me his ideas.

"We set up a haunted house in your basement," Simon began. We blindfold the kids and then lead them around to different spots. At each spot, we make them touch stuff and tell them what they're touching. Like we say that peeled grapes are eyeballs. We say cold spaghetti is ghoul guts and chicken bones are ribs and. . . ."

He would have gone on but I got the picture. And then I could picture all Ellen's dopey little friends. They'd be screaming and crying.

"Sounds good to me," I told him.

I didn't know if Simon's plan would sound good to my mom. Then again, she was the one who put me in charge. What she didn't know wouldn't hurt her.

Simon and I had until Saturday to get ready.

First, we cleared out the basement. Then we hung lots of spooky stuff — you know, skeletons that glow in the dark, bats in the air, that kind of stuff. Then, on the day of the party, we set up a bunch of tables. We got out all the things we wanted the girls to touch. I decided to dress up as a monster and jump out every now and then. What's Halloween without a good scream or two?

The girls all arrived after lunch on Saturday. Maybe that wasn't a good thing, I thought. I was sure a couple of them were going to lose their lunch.

Bonus!

I put on some spooky music in the basement. Then I went up and put on my monster outfit.

Simon was wearing a Count Dracula costume. He told Ellen to bring her friends downstairs.

"Von't you come in, beautiful ladies," Simon said in his best vampire voice. "Do not be afraid of my castle. I vant to be your friend. Heh, heh, heh."

He put blindfolds on the girls and led them around to the tables.

"This is blood," he said. One girl stuck her hand in ketchup. "I drink blood. Heh, heh, heh! I vant to drink *your* blood. Heh, heh, heh!"

She screamed. Way to go, Simon!

"This is a brain," he said. Another kid touched a cauliflower.

I jumped up from behind a chair and let out a scream.

All the little girls screamed right back. Then they ran upstairs.

We waited.

"Hey, Ellen!" I shouted. "Get your gutless little friends down here!"

But the only person who came downstairs was my mother.

"What's going on?" she demanded. "Why are all the girls crying?"

Then she looked around and figured it out.

"Sam, what's all this scary stuff? You were supposed to play Pass the Pumpkin. You were supposed to play pin the hat on the witch. I mean, these girls are only six years old!"

"So?" I said to her. "Halloween is supposed to be scary."

I could see my mom was ready to let out a scream herself. Simon and I hurried upstairs first.

We tried to calm the girls down. We got out the cake and ice cream and tried to get them to sing "Happy Birthday". But the girls were still crying. A couple of them just wanted to leave. Some of them had phoned home and were waiting at the door.

Then Ellen walked right up and kicked me in the shin again.

"You creep!" she yelled. "You're going to pay for this!"

I didn't know it then, but she was right.

CHAPTER 3

Into the Graveyard

I t didn't take long for word to get around.

When Simon and I went to the park, a bunch of guys were there. These guys were the big brothers of Ellen's friends. They were older than us, and bigger than us. And they were looking for a fight.

"Well, well, well," said this one huge, fat kid. "If it ain't the babysitters club."

I didn't know the kid's name, but I knew he was in grade nine. I knew he was really tough. And I knew he was really mean.

"Look," I started to say.

"No, you look," the kid said. He kept poking me in the chest. "You guys scared a bunch of little kids. My sister's still crying. So what are you going to do about it?"

I looked at Simon. For a second, I thought he might fall on his knees. Instead he spoke in a tiny voice. "We're sorry," said Simon. "We didn't mean to scare them. It was a Halloween party. We were just having fun with them."

"Yeah," said the fat kid. "And now we're going to have some fun with you."

I looked around the park. There were lots of people there. There was nothing these creeps could do with people watching us.

"Like right now?" I asked.

"Like tonight, dork," the fat kid said, poking me again. "What are you two losers doing tonight?"

"Well, we're taking Sam's. . . ." Simon began.

I knew what Simon was going to say. We were supposed to take Ellen trick or treating. I promised my mother. But if Fatso found out, we'd really look

like dorks. So I stomped on Simon's foot to shut him up.

"Ow!" yelled Simon.

I glared at the fat kid. "Why tonight?" I asked. "What's the big hurry?"

Fatso came over to me and breathed on me. Yuck. I think he'd just eaten a bag of garlic nachos.

"Here's what you're doing tonight," he said. "You two dorks are meeting me and my friends in the graveyard. Ten o'clock. Just inside the gate. We'll see how much you like being scared."

Then Fatso and his gang took off.

Simon watched them run off, then turned to me. "We don't have to go, Sam," he said. "We don't have to do what they say."

I rolled my eyes.

"Of course we have to go," I told him. "If we don't get this over with, they'll be after us every day. We'll never know when they're going to pull something."

"Okay," said Simon. I knew he didn't like this, but he'd always back me up. "How are we going to get out of the house?"

"We'll get out the way we always get out," I said. "I'll tell my parents I'm going to your house. You tell your parents you're coming to my house. They'll never know. We'll leave as soon as we're done taking Ellen around."

As it turned out, we didn't have to take Ellen trick or treating. My parents said they didn't trust me. Go figure. So they went out with her and I stayed home and handed out candy. My mom said to give every kid two of those little chocolate bars.

Yeah, right. I gave the trick-or-treat kids one bar and ate the second one myself. Who'd know?

As soon as my parents got home, I said I was going over to Simon's house. "He's rented some Halloween movies," I told them. "I'll probably be up late."

"Phone when you're on your way home," my dad said.

Uh-oh.

"Yeah . . . or . . . maybe I might sleep over at Simon's," I said. "I mean, if it's really late, I don't want to bother you."

"Well, phone and let us know before midnight," said my mom.

Yeah, right. I knew couldn't phone anybody from the graveyard.

"Well, how about I just sleep over at Simon's and then I won't have to phone." I didn't wait for an answer. "I'll grab my stuff."

I ran upstairs. Never give parents a chance to think. That's one thing I've learned.

"Don't forget your toothbrush," yelled my mom.

"I know you've been eating tons of those chocolate bars!"

What?! Did she have spy cameras on me?

I ran to Simon's house, but I didn't get inside.

"Sam!" Simon hissed from the bushes. "Over here! I told my parents I was watching movies at your house. I said I was sleeping over."

We snuck around to Simon's backyard and crept into the Bat House. We both ditched our pajamas and toothbrushes.

"Okay," I said. "What's the plan?"

"It's only 8:30," Simon said. "Maybe we should get over to the graveyard early. Then we can take a look around. Maybe we can spy on Fatso and see what he's up to."

"Good idea," I said. Just when I think Simon is a total dork, he comes up with stuff like that. *Check out the graveyard early!* I mean, that's brilliant.

We grabbed a couple of flashlights and pulled on dark sweatshirts. Then we hopped the backyard fence and took off down Maple Street. There were lots of kids still out, so no one looked at us. It took

us about ten minutes to get to the graveyard on Parker Drive.

"Now what?" asked Simon.

I knew we couldn't just walk in the front gate. There'd be a watchman on duty, for sure.

"Let's go down this side street," I said. "Maybe we can hop the fence somewhere."

Simon and I walked for about a block down one side of the graveyard. Then we saw a few bushes and I stopped. I pretended to tie up my shoe. When no cars were coming, Simon and I ran for the fence and hopped it. We fell into the bushes and stayed there for a couple of minutes.

"Now, let's sneak back to the front gate and wait for Fatso," Simon said. "We'll follow him around and see what he's got planned."

"Right," I replied.

I should have said *wrong*, but who knew?

CHAPTER 4

Chased by a Ghoul!

Simon and I worked our way back to the front of the graveyard. We found some bushes in front of a big tombstone and sat down to wait. I sure hoped *Mrs. Mary Jones, Loving Wife and Mother* didn't mind. We were sitting on her grave.

"What time is it?" I whispered.

Simon looked at his watch. It was one of those real fancy watches that tell you the time to the nanosecond.

"It's 9:42:05:43," he told me.

"Couldn't you just tell me it's twenty to ten?" I complained.

I looked around for the tenth time. "And why hasn't Fatso shown up? What's he going to do? Just walk in the front gate and expect us to be scared?"

We sat and waited and waited. We heard an owl hooting. Then we heard another owl hooting a little further off.

I looked at Simon.

"Those owls sound funny," he whispered.

I nodded. "I don't think those are owls, Simon."

"You think it's Fatso?" he whispered.

"Yeah, Fatso," I sighed. "And his friends."

"That means they're all here and hiding. Maybe they've been watching us all along."

I looked at the front gate. "We could just leave," I said.

"No way," said Simon. "You were right the first time. We either face up to them now or . . . "

"Spend the whole year waiting for them to do something awful," I finished for him. The choice was simple. "Let's just start walking and see what happens."

Simon and I stepped out from our hiding spot. We followed the path to the right. It led deeper and deeper into the graveyard. As the path got further and further away from the street, it got darker and darker.

"Hoot, hoot," called a very sick owl. Or one of Fatso's friends.

Okay. So they were watching us. They knew we were here. We just had to be ready for something to happen.

"Just keep walking, Simon," I whispered. "Don't look afraid."

So, we kept going. By now I didn't know where we were. Little paths just kept branching off from each other. We were deep in the heart of the graveyard. I couldn't even hear any road noises. But then I heard something that made my heart thump.

A dog growled. Then the dog barked.

Simon and I froze.

The barking got louder and louder. And let me tell you, this dog didn't sound like one of those little teacup poodles. This dog sounded like a cross between a Great Dane and a St. Bernard.

"Run!" I yelled to Simon.

Simon took off. I followed him. The dog was on our heels but I was too afraid to look back. I didn't want to see what a hound from hell looks like.

We ran and ran, twisting and turning. The dog was always just behind us. He kept growling like he'd tear us apart.

And then, suddenly, the barking stopped. I turned to look, but nothing was there. Then I turned back to Simon.

He wasn't there, either.

"Simon," I whispered. Then, "Simon," a little bit louder.

Where was he? Had the dog gotten him? Had the dog circled around me and come at Simon from the front? Was Simon now a chew toy?

I stood there in the dark for a few minutes, looking in every direction. I was afraid to move in case Simon came back. Then I heard a twig snap.

Someone was out there.

"Who's there?" I called. "Simon? Is that you?"

I heard another twig snap.

Then I remembered my flashlight. I yanked it out of my pocket and shone it all around.

I wished I hadn't.

The thing was only a few feet away. It was a ghoul, a ghoul dripping blood. The thing was huge, towering over me.

I turned and ran. The ghoul followed me. *Stupid!* I said to myself. *Turn off the flashlight!* I shoved it in my pocket. The thing was still following me, even in the dark. Then I heard the dog again. The dog was growling like he was about to jump on me.

I ran and ran. I couldn't see where I was going.

I didn't see the grave up ahead. I banged into the tombstone and tripped. I landed on something soft. The soft thing gave way and I was falling, down and down. Then I landed with a thud.

At last, I heard laughing. Crazy, evil laughing.

And then nothing.

I waited and waited. At last I turned on my flashlight to see where I was.

There was earth all around me. The hole was just a little bigger than I was — maybe two metres deep. Make that six feet deep.

Six feet deep.

Six feet deep!

I was in a grave.

CHAPTER 5

Buried Alive

I was in a freshly dug grave. All that was missing was a body. I figured there would be a funeral tomorrow. Great. The sad family comes to the gravesite and I'm there to say hello. Can you go to jail for that?

I was wedged into a corner, sitting on a canvas tarp that was bunched up around me. The tarp must have been the soft stuff I felt. I guessed the graveyard guys had covered the hole after they dug it. They'd take the tarp off just before the service.

I pulled at the tarp and noticed a plank of wood underneath. Hey! Maybe I could lean the plank against the side of the grave and crawl out. I stood up and felt pain shoot through my leg. I sat down fast. After a couple of minutes, I tried to stand up again. I put some weight on my foot. I could do it, but just barely. So maybe I hadn't broken anything, but my foot sure hurt.

I sat back down and rubbed my ankle. I could smell the earth all around me. Damp, musty, old. I knew it was full of worms and bugs and bones.

I shuddered. I did *not* want to be here. This was *too* much Halloween. This was Halloween for real.

I grabbed the plank and lifted it up. I put it against the side of the hole. Then I hopped over on my good foot and began to crawl up the plank. I wobbled a bit and fell to the side. Ow! Maybe I'd have to wait down here for help. But then I thought about the next day — all this dirt falling down on me, burying me alive. So I tried again. This time I went more slowly and watched my balance. I was almost out when I heard a noise. Voices. Was it Fatso? The ghoul? Simon?

I couldn't really see over the top of the grave. I didn't know what to do. Should I make a run for it? But what about my foot? Would I be able to get that far? What if it was Fatso and he caught me? What if it was the ghoul out there, waiting for me?

I decided to stay in the grave. I slid back down the plank and knocked it to one side. Then I covered myself with the tarp. I figured I'd find out who it was first, and then call for help.

I sat there and listened. I could hear talking,

and then I could hear something being dragged. Someone grunted. Someone swore. The guy didn't sound like Fatso. He sounded old, real old, like my dad. I was glad I'd stayed put.

They were above me now.

"Are you sure about this?"

"You changing your mind?"

"The funeral's tomorrow. They'll find him right away. Yeah. Maybe we should have tossed him in the lake. Then maybe no one would ever find him."

"I *want* them to find him. I want to teach them a lesson. The sooner the better. Hear what I'm saying?"

"I hear you," said the first voice. Then he changed his tone. "Poor Tony. Should have kept his mouth shut."

"Yeah. My heart's bleeding. Now dump him."

I heard a couple of grunts. Then something big and heavy landed on me. I felt the breath go out of me. I almost made a sound, but I clamped my hand over my mouth.

"Tomorrow, we know nothing. Hear what I'm

saying?"

"I hear you, boss."

They moved away, but I sat there frozen. I don't know how long I waited. Too bad Simon wasn't around with his watch to tell me.

Finally, I tried to shove the thing off me. Then I crawled, wincing with pain, out from under the tarp.

I didn't want to look at the thing, but I had to.

It was a man. The man's eyes bugged out and his tongue rolled out of his mouth.

I'd never seen a dead body before, but I was pretty sure I was seeing one now. I was pretty sure this was Tony.

And I was really sure I was going to be sick.

CHAPTER 6

Rescue!

I wasn't just *going* to be sick. I *was* sick. Throwing up isn't pretty. But that wasn't all. As I wiped my mouth on my sleeve, I felt something sticky and wet. I touched it with my finger and then held it up to the moonlight. Blood! I was sure it was blood — Tony's blood!

I yanked off my sweatshirt and threw it down. I didn't look at the dead man again. In books and movies it's fun when something like this happens.

It's not so fun when it happens in real life. I have to tell you, I was scared.

I pulled out the plank and propped it back up again. Then I pushed and pulled myself up, trying not to cry out when I jabbed my foot. I didn't care if there was a ghoul sitting there waiting for me. I was getting out of this hole. I was getting away from this dead body. For once, I wanted to be home and in bed.

I crawled over the top and dragged myself to the trees a few metres away. Then I sat with my back against a pine and tried to figure out what to do. Maybe I could hop to the front gate. But I was lost and didn't know my way back. Maybe I'd have to stay here until someone showed up for work in the morning. I didn't want to stay in this place one more nanosecond, but maybe I didn't have a choice.

And then I heard something. I froze. My heart started to pound. Not again, I thought. *Nothing more, please, please, please,* I begged silently.

"Sam? Sam? Are you there?"

It was Simon!

"Simon!" I shouted. "Over here! Help!"

Simon rushed over to me.

"What happened to you? Where have you been?"

"Where have *I* been?! Where have *you* been?" I shot back at him. "I needed you, buddy. Where were you?!"

"I was running from the dog, and I thought you were right behind me. When I looked back, you weren't there. I hid behind some bushes, on the lookout for you. Then I saw Fatso and his friends."

"You saw those guys? What were they doing?" I asked.

"One of them was dressed up in a lame costume," Simon said. "A giant monster, dripping blood. Real stupid. But then the others helped him get up on some stilts and off he went back the way we had come. Did you see him?"

"Uh, yeah, I saw him," I mumbled. So maybe I was dumb to be so scared, but no way I'd admit that. "Real lame," I said. "Didn't fool me," I lied.

Simon nodded. "So I followed those guys for awhile, but then I stepped on something." Simon held up a small recorder. "Listen," he said. He pressed the On button and suddenly a dog was barking like crazy.

"It was *them*?" I sighed. "The recorder was the dog!"

"Yeah," said Simon. "They chased us through the graveyard blasting this tape. Pretty cool, huh? I mean, they really did scare us, didn't they?" He started to laugh.

I nodded. But I didn't laugh quite so hard.

"Well, I followed the guys a bit more. I guess they'd lost both of us, so they left the graveyard. I saw them hop a fence. Then I went back and looked for you. But I got lost, and, well . . . sorry it took me so long."

So then I told Simon what had happened to me. I fudged the first bit. No need for Simon to know I just about peed my pants when I saw the ghoul.

But I didn't leave anything out about the grave.

And when I was finished, Simon just sat staring at me.

"Wow!" he whispered. "Wow!"

"What are we going to do?" I asked.

"We have to go to the police," Simon replied. "That body . . . I mean, you must have seen a mob hit, or something."

I'd seen *The Godfather*. I knew what happened to people who ran into the mob.

"What if we have to go into hiding?" I asked. "What if we have to leave home and change our names? What if we never get to talk to our families again? What if we can't even talk to each other?"

Simon sat thinking. I knew he was thinking hard because he has this thing he does when he thinks. He closed his eyes and screwed up his face. Then he burst out, "Sam! You didn't *see* the hit! You didn't *see* who did it! You just had a body thrown on top of you. We can go to the police and tell them to look in the grave. You're not a witness to anything!"

"You're right! I don't even have to tell them I

44

looked at the body. I can say it was covered with the tarp. And I don't have to tell them his name is . . . was . . . Tony. They can figure all that out for themselves."

Simon pulled me up and helped me hobble to the front gate.

But then I had a brainstorm.

"Simon! I don't have to say anything! They're going to bury some guy tomorrow. They're going to find the body then. They don't need to know I was here."

Simon thought for a bit. Once again he closed his eyes and screwed up his face.

"I think you're right," he said at last. "This could get you in a lot of trouble."

So Simon and I made it back to my house. We snuck in my back door and then went down to the basement to sleep.

I breathed a sigh of relief. I was home, safe and sound . . . I thought.

CHAPTER 7

Nothing but the Truth . . . Sort Of

In the morning, Simon helped me up the stairs. We were in the kitchen eating cereal when my mom came down.

I showed her my ankle. It was swollen and all black and purple.

"What happened?" she asked.

"Uh . . . I sort of fell at Simon's," I said. "You know, out of the Bat House."

"But why didn't you tell me? It looks bad."

"Uh . . . I didn't want to wake you," I answered.

My mom sighed. "I'll have a quick shower," she said. "Then I'll take you to the hospital." She left the room and Simon and I kept eating.

Then, all of a sudden, we heard a siren. Then more sirens. All those sirens were coming down my street. Simon jumped up to look out the window.

"Wow!" he yelled, "three cop cars and . . ." He stopped and swung around to look at me. "They're coming here! They stopped right in front of your house."

In a second there was some loud banging on the front door.

"Hide!" I shouted.

Simon looked at me like I was nuts.

My dad hurried down the stairs in his pajamas and opened the door.

"We're looking for Sam Fletcher," said one cop.

Then the cop saw me.

"Are you Sam Fletcher?" he asked. "Is this your sweatshirt?"

I stared at the sweatshirt. The one with vomit

on the front and blood on the sleeve.

"Um . . . ah . . . I'm not sure," I mumbled.

"We found your wallet in the pocket. Sam Fletcher — is that you? Yes or no?"

"What's this all about?" asked my dad. "What's going on?"

The cop turned to my dad. "Sir, this sweatshirt was found at a crime scene. The wallet inside says Sam Fletcher, 34 Pinehill Avenue. This is 34 Pinehill. Is Sam Fletcher your boy?"

My dad glared at me. "Sam, what have you done now?" he sighed.

I didn't know what to tell him. I couldn't tell the truth. The truth was too messy, too crazy. But what lie could I tell? Simon and I hadn't thought this far ahead.

But I didn't have to say anything.

"Wait a minute," said another cop. "I know you, don't I? You're the kid who caught that drug dealer at the school. Right? Last month? You and . . ." He turned to look at Simon. "And you!"

"Yes, sir. Yes, we are," said Simon.

"Okay," said the second cop. "So I know you two might have been up to something last night. But I don't think you killed anybody."

"Killed somebody?!" shrieked my dad.

"Why don't we go down to the police station?" suggested the nice cop. "Maybe we can figure this whole thing out."

"Are we under arrest?" Simon asked.

"Cool," I said.

"Nah, we just want to talk to you," said the first cop. Then he turned to speak to my dad, "Sir, you can follow us in your own car."

I stood up and hobbled behind the police. Two of them looked at my foot and shook their heads. "We can hardly wait to hear your story, son," said the nice one.

So Simon and I got into the squad car.

"I'll call your parents," my dad yelled to Simon. "We'll be right behind you."

It wasn't a long ride to the station. But with the cops in the car with us, Simon and I didn't have a chance to talk about our story. What were we going to say?

We got out of the car and one of the cops helped me inside. Then he took us to a room and told us to sit down.

"I'm Officer Bing," he said. "And I want the truth. You two are involved in something very serious."

I nodded. I'd made up my mind. I would tell the truth, the whole truth, nothing but the truth.

That's what they say on TV. It was good enough for me.

Just then, another officer came into the room.

"This is Sgt. Melly," said Officer Bing. "He's very interested in what you're going to tell us."

I nodded. Then I started to talk. I told them all about Ellen's party and about Fatso. I told them about going to the graveyard. I told them about being chased by the dog and the giant ghoul. Then I told them about falling into the grave.

"Now this part is very important," said Sgt. Melly. "Hear what I'm saying? I want you to be very careful about this next part. Don't leave anything out."

I stared at him. My heart started to pound.

"N . . . n . . . no, sir," I mumbled.

But of course, I did leave something out.

I told the police that I was so scared I threw up. All over my sweatshirt. So I pulled it off and left it there. I told them how I saw the plank and crawled out. Then I told them that Simon found me and helped me home.

"And that's all. Honest," I said. "I don't know

anything about a body."

Sgt. Melly sat down in front of me. He put his hand under my chin and turned my face towards his. He looked me right in the eye.

"You're sure, Sam? Nothing else to tell us?"

I gulped and nodded. "I'm sure, sir," I said.

"It will be bad for you if you're lying to me, Sam. *Hear what I'm saying?*" he asked.

I nodded again.

"I hear you," I said. But I was certain I'd heard those words and that voice before.

CHAPTER 8

Betrayal! Or Lyayrtub!

Sgt. Melly didn't take his eyes off me.

"Good," he said. "Now what's all this about a body?"

I stared at him.

"A body?" I said. My voice was shaking.

"That's right," replied Sgt. Melly "You said you didn't know about a body. Now, who told you this had anything to do with a body?"

I didn't know what to say. My mouth went dry and my hands started sweating. I wanted to look away from Sgt. Melly, but I couldn't. I felt like I was a small animal staring into the eyes of a cobra. I felt like I was about to be eaten alive.

And then Simon broke in. "But the cops were talking about it. They told us someone had been killed. We just *figured* there was a body."

Sometimes Simon is the best friend a guy could have.

Sgt. Melly looked away from me and turned to Simon. "You're the smart one, aren't you?" he said.

"I try, sir," Simon replied.

"Get out of here, both of you," said Sgt. Melly "Go on home. But if you think of anything, I want you to tell me. Hear what I'm saying?"

Simon and I got out of there as fast as we could. I knew Simon was dying to talk to me, but our parents were all over us. The next couple of hours were a little crazy. My parents took me to the hospital. Then they yelled at me the whole time the doctor was checking out my foot. I had sprained my ankle, so the hospital gave me crutches to use for a few days. I wished they had given me earplugs, too.

When I got home, I was grounded. Not that I minded. I needed a weekend locked in my house. No way I was going outside after what had happened. In fact, maybe I'd just stay in my room forever.

I was just reading a comic book when Ellen knocked on my door.

"I brought you a note from Simon," she said.

I grabbed the note from her. This is what Simon and I do when we're grounded. The note was in our Bat Code. This means you change the vowels around, like this.

A E I O U Y

Y U O I E A

So my name, Sam, is Sym. Except to make it harder, you write the word backwards. So Sam is Mys. Simon is Nimos.

Simon wrote, "Ahw dod eia uol?"

I wrote a note back. "O dyh it. To syw moh. Allum."

— Why did you lie?
— I had to. It was him. Melly.

56

I called Ellen.

"You have to pay a dollar," she said.

I gave her the money and waited. Sure enough, she was back in a few minutes, with another note.

Simon wrote, "Allum? O t'nid tug to."

So I gave Ellen another dollar and sent back another note. "Allum syw ty uht dryauvyrg. O dryuh moh."

Soon, I had another note from Simon. "Hyua, thgor."

I was so mad, I didn't send another note. Did Simon think I had made this up? I knew it was Melly. He was the one called Boss.

The next day was Monday, and my mom said she'd drive me to school.

"But I'm grounded," I said. "I can't go to school."

"Don't be an idiot," said my mom. "You're only

Melly? I don't get it.

Melly was at the graveyard. I heard him.

Yeah, right.

57

grounded evenings and weekends. Of course you're going to school."

I tried begging. "Please mom. Pleeeeeze. Don't make me go. I can't leave the house. I just can't. Pleeeeeze."

"What's the matter with you, Sam? Here's your lunch. Get in the car."

Simon was waiting for me in the schoolyard. He looked all around to make sure no one was listening.

"Are you nuts?" he whispered. "It can't be Sgt. Melly."

"Was too," I said. "I heard him. He kept saying 'hear what I'm saying' at the graveyard. And he said it to us yesterday, too. So there."

"Are you sure?" Simon asked.

"Sure I'm sure. I felt sick as soon as he started talking to me. It was him all right."

"We have to tell somebody," said Simon.

I nodded.

"We have to tell a cop," said Simon.

"Sgt. Melly is a cop," I reminded him.

And then Simon did that thing he does when he's thinking. He closed his eyes and screwed up his face.

"Officer Brannon!" he shouted.

Officer Brannon had helped us catch the drug dealer last month. She knows us. She might just believe us.

"Good plan," I said.

We had to wait a whole week — until I could walk again — and my mom wasn't driving me back

59

and forth. Then Simon and I went to the police station one night after supper. In a few minutes, we were with Officer Brannon.

"So I hear you boys have been in trouble again, eh?" she said.

"Big trouble," I answered.

"What do you mean?" she asked.

"You won't believe this," I said.

"I don't even believe it," said Simon.

"Shut up," I told him. "It's the truth."

Then I told Officer Brannon about what really happened at the graveyard. I told her about the dead body. I told her about Sgt. Melly.

She looked at me as if I had two heads. "This is crazy," she said.

"It's the truth," I repeated.

She sat there thinking for a while, not talking to us. Then she got up. "Wait right here," she said and left the room.

In a few minutes she came back.

And behind her was Sgt. Melly.

CHAPTER 9

Tricks. No Treats.

I jumped up.

"What are you doing?!" I yelled. "Why is he here?!"

"Tell him, Sam," Officer Brannon said. "Tell Sgt. Melly what you just told me."

But I couldn't say anything. No words would come out of my mouth.

Officer Brannon gave me a dirty look.

"Lost your nerve? Afraid to tell Sgt. Melly what you told me?"

"What are you saying?" My voice sounded like a croak. "Why are you doing this?"

In no time Officer Brannon told Sgt. Melly what I had told her.

"But you don't have any proof, do you Sam?" she asked. "You're just trying to look important. You're just making up stuff, aren't you?"

"But I do have . . ." I began.

"Shut up, Sam," ordered Officer Brannon. "I've had enough of your lies."

Sgt. Melly was looking at me.

"He's just a kid," said Officer Brannon. "He's just a stupid little jerk who thinks he can solve crimes. Let's forget about it."

"Oh, I will," said Sgt. Melly. "Beat it, Sam. You too, Simon. I don't ever want to see you two again. Hear what I'm saying? I'm going to let you both off this time. But don't you dare pull a stunt like this again."

"You heard him," said Officer Brannon. "Get out. Lucky for you I won't call your parents."

Simon and I ran out of the room. We ran out of

the building. We would have kept running but my foot started to hurt. We sat down on a bench.

"Now what?" asked Simon.

"It was him," I said. "And now he knows that we know."

"Ah, knock it off, Sam. He's a cop. He didn't kill anybody."

I didn't say a word. I stood up.

"Where are you going?" Simon asked.

"Get lost," I told him.

I started for home, but it was going to take a long time with my foot hurting. I took the short-cut through the park. In no time, I heard someone running behind me.

"I'm coming with you," Simon said.

"It's a free country," I said, still mad.

We walked for a bit, keeping to the park road. It was dark, but not pitch dark. Between the moon and the park lights, we could see pretty well. Once I stumbled and Simon grabbed my arm and held me up. I shook him off and kept walking.

I heard a car. It wasn't going fast, but it was

coming up behind me. I turned to look. Why didn't it have its headlights on?

Then I heard the squeal of tires. Suddenly the headlights were on, blinding me. I wanted to run, but I couldn't. I just stood there, waiting to be hit.

And then I saw Simon leap across the road and into the glare of the lights. He grabbed me and pushed me out of the way. I landed on the grass, my bad leg screaming out in pain. Then Simon was by my side, yanking me up.

"Run!" he screamed.

I heard tires squeal again and the headlights found us. The driver raced the engine and came up over the curb. He was gunning for us again!

But all of a sudden, there were more headlights. Two cars crashed into the one chasing us. Then lots of car doors opened and slammed shut.

What was going on?!

"Get out of the car, Melly!" someone ordered. "Keep your hands up where we can see them!"

I watched as Sgt. Melly got out of the car. A whole bunch of cops circled around him. Then

I saw Officer Brannon put handcuffs on him. She pushed him into a police car.

Simon crawled over to me.

"Sam! Are you alright?"

I looked at Simon. I didn't know what was happening, but I knew Simon had saved my life. I owed him big time.

Officer Brannon came over and helped me up.

"Sorry about that, guys," she said. "I hope you weren't too scared."

Scared? Me? I just about pooped my pants and she wanted to know if I was scared?

"See, we had a hunch that Melly was a bad cop. We could never get anything on him. Until today. Not until you walked in with your story, Sam."

"I don't get it," I said. "Why did you bring in Melly like that? You saw how mad he was at me."

Officer Brannon smiled at me. "Exactly. We set him up. And we set you up too. I'm sorry, Sam. I wanted him to know you'd heard him at the graveyard. I wanted him to think that you were a witness. But I wanted him to think I didn't believe you."

"That much makes sense," Simon replied.

"Anyhow, I figured he'd follow you," Brannon went on. "And I was right. We kept following him following you," she explained. "You weren't in any real danger."

Sure. Tell that to my underpants!

Sharon Jennings is the author of more than fifteen books for young people. Her first success was a picture book, *Jeremiah and Mrs. Ming*, illustrated by Mireille Levert. Since then, Sharon has written five other picture books, including *Priscilla and Rosy* and *Priscilla's Pas de Deux*, both illustrated by Linda Hendry.

Sharon has already created four books about the Bat Gang: *Bats and Burglars, Bats in the Garbage, Bats out the Window* and *Bats Past Midnight*. This book is her fifth "Bats" novel.

Sharon says, "There is nothing I like to do more than write. I become the characters and live inside their story." In real life, Sharon Jennings balances her writing life with being a mother of two sons and a daughter. She lives in Toronto but frequently visits schools across Canada and in the United States. For more information, visit her website at www.sharonjennings.ca.